To Ken Wilson, for being a great and not-so-little brother.
And to Garth Holden and Sheri Radford, for suggesting some
great and not-so-little revisions. —T.W.

Dedicated to my nieces and nephews: Bodhi, Dryden,
Willow, and Marcus. —J.H.

Text © 2017 Troy Wilson
Illustrations © 2017 Josh Holinaty

Owlkids Books acknowledges the financial support of the Canada Council for the Arts, the Ontario Arts Council,
the Government of Canada through the Canada Book Fund (CBF) and the Government of Ontario through
the Ontario Media Development Corporation's Book Initiative for our publishing activities.

Published in Canada by Owlkids Books Inc.
10 Lower Spadina Avenue, Toronto, ON M5V 2Z2

Published in the United States by Owlkids Books Inc.
1700 Fourth Street, Berkeley, CA 94710

Library and Archives Canada Cataloguing in Publication

Wilson, Troy, 1970-, author
Liam takes a stand / written by Troy Wilson ; illustrated by Josh Holinaty.

ISBN 978-1-77147-161-9 (hardback)

I. Holinaty, Josh, illustrator II. Title.

PS8645.I48L53 2017   jC813'.6   C2016-904288-X

Library of Congress Control Number: 2016946653

Edited by: Jessica Burgess and Karen Li
Designed by: Alisa Baldwin

Manufactured in Dongguan, China, in November 2016, by Toppan Leefung Packaging & Printing (Dongguan) Co., Ltd.
Job #BAYDC29

A   B   C   D   E   F

ONTARIO ARTS COUNCIL
CONSEIL DES ARTS DE L'ONTARIO
an Ontario government agency
un organisme du gouvernement de l'Ontario

Canada Council   Conseil des Arts
for the Arts   du Canada

Canada

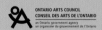

 Publisher of Chirp, chickaDEE and OWL   Owlkids Books is a division of   Bayard
www.owlkidsbooks.com   CANADA

Lister and Lester were identical twins who did identical things.

When Lister joined the track team, Lester came running.
When Lester joined the swim team, Lister dove in, too.
And they both rocked the art club at exactly the same time.

**They were constantly competing
with each other.**

Sometimes Lister won, and sometimes Lester won.
But their little brother, Liam?

Liam *never* won.

Mostly, he just wanted to play with them.
But Lister and Lester didn't have time for that.

On the first day of summer, Lester's Lemonade Universe opened for business. Lister's Lemonade *Multi*verse opened right next door.

"Are you hiring?" asked Liam.

"I'll even work for free."

"You'd just slow me down," said Lister.

"You'd just hold me up," said Lester.

Liam was discouraged. But not for long.
"I'll show them how hard I can work!" he thought.

So he did odd jobs around the neighborhood.

Everyone paid him in cash.
Except Mrs. Redmond, who paid him in apples.

And that inspired a plan. "Maybe . . . "
he thought, "at just the right time . . . "

Back at the stands, Lester called his lemonade
NEW AND IMPROVED (when he added bigger ice cubes).

Lister claimed his lemonade would make you run fast
(if you drank fifty glasses).

Lister started selling pink lemonade.

Lester started selling purple.

Lester blasted music.

Lister hired a band.

They spent all their earnings
on bigger and crazier gimmicks.

Liam, on the other hand, mostly saved.
Everyone still paid him in cash.
Except Mrs. Redmond.

"Almost time . . ." he thought.

Lister bought ads (he borrowed the
money from their mom).
Lester bought billboards (he borrowed
the money from their dad).

They got more foot traffic.

More bike traffic.

More car, van, and truck traffic.
"This," thought Liam, "is just the right time!"
And so . . .

Liam's Apple Avenue opened for business.

His music was soft, and his smile was inviting.

He added a hint of ginger to his juice.

He sprinkled a dash of cinnamon.

He posted a sign that said

FRESH FROM THIS AVENUE'S FINEST APPLES.

"He won't last a week," said Lester.
"He won't last a day," said Lister.

But seven and a half
days later . . .

Liam had all the traffic.
And so . . .

Lister's Apple Highway opened for business.
Lester's Apple *Super*highway opened right next door.

At first, they left out the ginger and cinnamon.
Then they put in too much.

And their attempts to snare Liam's customers didn't help one bit.

They ran out of money and went out of business.
Even worse, they still owed money to their parents.

So they did odd jobs around the neighborhood.
The more they worked, the more they wondered . . .

"Should I?"

"Could I?"

Lister walked. Lester jogged.

Lester ran. Lister sprinted.

They asked Liam if he was hiring.

"You'd just slow me down," said Liam to Lister.

"You'd just hold me up," said Liam to Lester.

Lester hung his head. Lister hung his head and shoulders.

"I'm sorry," said Lister.

"I'm sorrier," said Lester.

"I'm sorriest," said Liam,

" . . . that we never have time to play."

"If you hire me," offered Lester, "I'll play
with you for an hour a week."
"If you hire me," offered Lister, "I'll play
with you for two hours a week."

"Five hours a week!" countered Lester.
"Seven hours a week!" countered Lister.
"Deal!" said Liam.

So they worked.

And played.

And played.
And worked.

And sometimes . . .